Sweet Dreams

To my favorite animal friends who love to sleep:
Olive the dog, Clemens the rabbit,
Feldspar the hamster, Peppy P. U. the guinea pig,
the Big Kahuna (world's fattest cat), Bean the frog,
Nana the human, and Christopher the human

Acknowledgments:
Academy of Natural Sciences, Bat Conservation International, Bronx Zoo/Wildlife Conservation Park, Conservation International, San Diego Zoo, Sea World of California, Bob Benson, Peter Blauner, Don Bruning, Ron Garrison, Brian Keely, Karen Killmar, Margaret Kinnard, Ginger Knowlton, Andrew Mack, Jeff Munson, Christy Ottaviano, Gary Priest, Dave Rimlinger, Valerie Thompson, and Debra Wright.

Permission for use of the following photographs is gratefully acknowledged:
Orangutan: Michael P. Turco / Lions: Zoological Society of San Diego, photo by Lyla and Arthur Emmrich / Shark: Innerspace Visions, photo by Mark Conlin / Black bears: Lynn and Donna Rogers / Koala: Zoological Society of San Diego, photo by Ron Gordon Garrison / Sea otter: Leonard Lee Rue III / Sloth: Kevin Schafer / Bat: Merlin D. Tuttle, Bat Conservation International / Hippopotamus: Zoological Society of San Diego, photo by Ron Gordon Garrison / Flamingos: Sea World, Inc., photo courtesy of Sea World of California / Chipmunk: Leonard Lee Rue III / Horses: Winston Fraser / Baby and mother human: Positive Images, photo by David Pratt / Girl with teddy bear: Grace Davies / Puppy: Evelyn Clarke Mott / Bear in tree: Virginia Grimes / Cat in bed: Evelyn Clarke Mott / Cat: Evelyn Clarke Mott / Hugging orangutans: Dan Polin

Henry Holt and Company, LLC, *Publishers since 1866,* 115 West 18th Street, New York, New York 10011

Henry Holt is a registered trademark of Henry Holt and Company, LLC

Published in Canada by Fitzhenry & Whiteside Ltd., 195 Allstate Parkway, Markham, Ontario L3R 4T8.

Library of Congress Cataloging-in-Publication Data
Kajikawa, Kimiko. Sweet dreams: how animals sleep / Kimiko Kajikawa. Summary: Rhyming verses followed by factual information briefly describe the sleep habits of a variety of animals. 1. Sleep behavior in animals— Juvenile literature. [1. Animals—Sleep behavior. 2. Sleep.] I. Title. QL755.3.K36 1999 591.5'19—dc21 98-16637

ISBN 0-8050-5890-7 / First Edition—1999 / Designed by Meredith Baldwin
Printed in the United States of America on acid-free paper. ∞
3 5 7 9 10 8 6 4 2

Sweet Dreams

★ How Animals Sleep ★

Kimiko Kajikawa

Henry Holt and Company ★ New York

ORANGUTANS

doze in a bed of leaves.

LIONS

sleep wherever they please.

SHARKS

rest with eyes open wide.

BLACK BEARS

go into dens and hide.

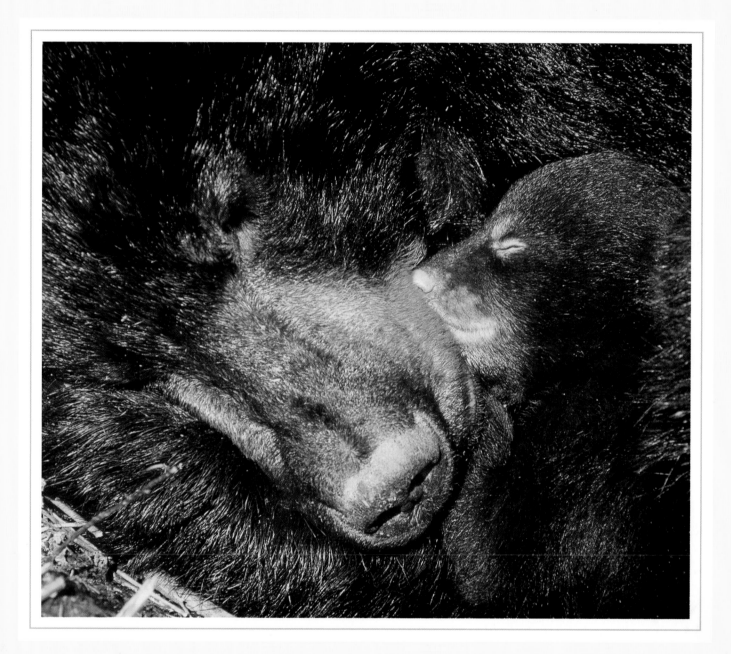

KOALAS

snooze up in trees.

SEA OTTERS

float on top of the sea.

SLOTHS

sleep most of the day and night.

BATS

hang upside down,
out of the light.

HIPPOS

pile in a great big heap.

FLAMINGOS

stand on one leg to sleep.

CHIPMUNKS

curl in a furry ball.

HORSES

stand up straight and tall.

Some people snore,
and some people talk.

Some sleep still,
and some sleepwalk.

Everyone sleeps in a
different way.

How will you
go to sleep today?

Orangutans Doze in a Bed of Leaves.

About a half hour before sunset, an orangutan builds a platform bed of branches and leaves in the fork of a tall tree. It needs only around ten minutes to do this—a good thing because an orangutan builds a new bed every night! An orangutan lies on its bed and locks its fingers and toes onto the tree's branches. If it rains during the night, the orangutan makes an umbrella by holding or placing large leaves around its head.

Lions Sleep Wherever They Please.

Because lions have no predators, they feel safe wherever they are. A lion will sleep flat on its back with all four paws sticking straight up. Some lions even sleep in trees. The lion is an excellent hunter and needs to spend only about two hours a day in search of food. The rest of the day and night it spends playing and dozing.

Sharks Rest with Eyes Open Wide.

A shark doesn't sleep like we do. It never closes its eyes to rest. Instead, it goes through resting cycles where it slows down its movements. The wide-eyed shark remains aware of sights, smells, and sounds, so it does not miss possible food, mates, or predators.

Black Bears Go into Dens and Hide.

To prepare for a long, cold winter, a black bear spends most of the fall fattening up. It builds a winter den in a hollow tree, rock cave, or brush pile. With strong claws, it makes a bed of dried leaves, grass, evergreens, and bark. When winter comes, the bear sleeps in its cozy bed. For up to seven months, it doesn't eat, drink, or go to the bathroom. Bears that live in warmer climates may hibernate for shorter periods of time, or not at all.

Koalas Snooze up in Trees.

Koalas are picky eaters—eating mostly leaves from certain types of eucalyptus trees. Because a koala is so fussy, it sleeps about fifteen hours and rests an additional five hours each day to save energy. Snuggled up on the high limbs of the eucalyptus tree, the koala snoozes most of the day away.

Sea Otters Float on Top of the Sea.

A sea otter sleeps flat on its back in the chilly coastal sea. It anchors itself in a bed of kelp, a kind of seaweed, to keep from drifting out into the ocean. Mother and pup hold paws to stay together while they sleep. During the day, a resting otter may place its paws over its eyes to block the sun.

Sloths Sleep Most of the Day and Night.

A sloth spends about twenty hours a day sleeping. The rest of the time, it moves very s-l-o-w-l-y or not at all. A sloth hooks itself onto a tree branch with its clawed toes and hangs upside down. In this position, it eats, mates, and sleeps. Some sloths spend their entire lives in the same tree.

Bats Hang Upside Down, Out of the Light.

Because they are active at night and sleep during the day, bats are called nocturnal. A tired bat finds a dark place and curls its toes around its roost. Hanging upside down, it cleans itself with its tongue. Then it folds its wings around its body and goes to sleep.

Hippos Pile in a Great Big Heap.

All day long, the hippopotamus sleeps in the river. Because it doesn't have sweat glands, resting in water keeps it cool and comfortable. A hippo can even sleep under the water, coming to the surface every few minutes for a breath of air. At night, hippos leave the river to munch on the grassy banks.

Flamingos Stand on One Leg to Sleep.

When a flamingo sleeps, it often stands in water on one leg and tucks its head under a wing. A resting flamingo almost always faces the wind. This stops the rain and wind from getting into its feathers. Standing on one leg, a flamingo sways back and forth with the breeze.

Chipmunks Curl in a Furry Ball.

During the warm months, a chipmunk stores nuts and seeds in its burrow, a small underground hole. When winter comes, the chipmunk enters the burrow, curls up in a furry ball, and falls asleep on a bed of dried grass and leaves. But the chipmunk is a light sleeper. Every now and then, it wakes up to have a snack or go to the bathroom. Then it falls back asleep and waits for spring.

Horses Stand Up Straight and Tall.

A horse stands up on its four legs, locks its joints in place, relaxes its muscles, and falls asleep. Because a standing horse can't move its legs when it sleeps, it can't dream. Dreaming requires muscle movement. Sometimes a horse will lie down on its side or stomach and dream, but most of the time, it sleeps standing up.

Some People Snore, and Some People Talk.
Some Sleep Still, and Some Sleepwalk.

Most people lie down at night, pull up their covers, close their eyes, and quietly sleep. As people get older, they need less sleep. Newborn babies sleep about seventeen hours a day and adults only about eight hours. During sleep, heartbeat and breathing slow down, muscles relax, and blood pressure falls. All people need sleep to stay healthy. Without it, they become cranky and moody and have difficulty concentrating. Sleep is rest for the body and mind.

Everyone Sleeps in a Different Way.
How Will You Go to Sleep Today?

Here are some questions to ask yourself:

★ Where do you like to sleep?

★ What is your favorite sleeping position?

★ Do you take naps during the day?

★ How many hours do you usually sleep at a time?

★ What kinds of sounds do you think you make while you sleep?

★ What is the funniest thing about the way you sleep?

How Long They Sleep
(Average Number of Hours per Day)

Hibernating black bear	24	Tree bat	12
Lion	20	Human child	11
Sloth	20	Chipmunk	9
Newborn human child	17	Human adult	8
Koala	15	Flamingo	6
Hippopotamus	14	Horse	5
Orangutan	12	Shark	unknown
Sea otter	12